From the autho

Autumn Reads

A selection of six short stories by
April E Swan

For my Mum, Ann – who has always wanted to write a book. Hopefully, one day you will.

A word from the author.

Over the past eight months, I have found myself on a very steep learning curve. I self-published my crime Novella 'Motive' and found that writing is not as easy as it looks. Who knew? Juggling a forty-hour working week, children, dogs, and a husband, whilst trying to write something people might actually want to read was a very tall order indeed. When you publish your work you make yourself very vulnerable. It is inevitable that you will get good and bad reviews, and that your writing won't be to everybody's taste. I am slowly learning to roll with the punches. A few months ago, my confidence was knocked, and I told myself I wasn't going to put myself through it all again. In fact, I actually said, 'I'm never writing another book again.'

And while, technically, 'Autumn Reads' isn't a novel, I did find myself itching to try different genres. I enjoy writing and creating something unique. This collection includes a science fiction story – Author No.3, a horror story – The Overnight Success, a thriller story – The Anger Issue, a romance story – Just Love Me, a fantasy story – The Wishing Tree, and Charlie Sprattel – the only story I haven't been able to assign a genre too. I will leave you to make your own mind up about his story.

So, snuggle up under a blanket. Grab a warm drink, and enjoy some precious 'You time' with Autumn Reads. Autumn is my favourite season. I love nothing more than reading a good book, curled up nice and warm, and listening to the rain outside.

Contents

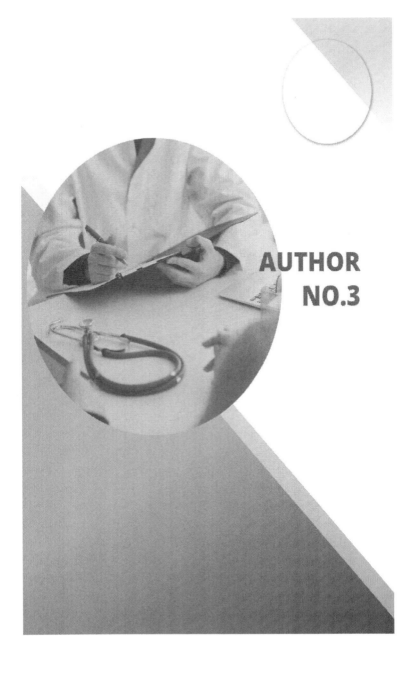

AUTHOR NO.3

In between New Browning and Heathcote, there is a human body research laboratory tucked away behind four-metre-high palisade fencing that displays a huge white and yellow metal sign. The sign reads **'PRIVATE PROPERTY NO TRESPASSING – TRESPASSERS WILL BE PROSECUTED.'** The Testing Grounds of Somatology (TGS) laboratory is twenty-five stories high, with large windows adorned by grey slat blinds. The exterior brickwork is an uninteresting grey colour, and the building never seems to catch the sunlight. It looks like any other research facility, and anyone who passed by would assume that hundreds of scientists are inside, busy finding cures for terminal illnesses.

Late at night, inside the TGS laboratory, there is only one scientist at work. Dr. Earl Morris walks along a brightly lit, white-walled corridor toward room 209. His new white trainers squeak as he walks across the grey anti-microbial linoleum floor. His white coat falls just above the knees of his denim jeans. He scratches his stubbled chin before swiping his key card into the lock and opening the door to room 209.

He picks up a clipboard from a large, white desk in the far corner of the room, and removes a biro pen from the top pocket of his white coat. His green eyes flick from left to right as he reviews the test results from last night's experiment. He bites on his dry, upper lip as he reads, and wipes a bead of sweat from his forehead. He finds it difficult to concentrate with a gun pointed directly at his head.

After studying Biochemistry at University, Earl moved on to a Ph.D. in the study of social behaviours in mice. A promising young scientist, with an impeccable reputation, he hadn't thought that the one mistake he made when he was fifteen would catch up with him. He hadn't realised that anyone even knew. The threatening text messages had started about a

1

month ago. When they first started, they simply said 'I know what you did' and 'You can't ignore me for much longer.' He had replied to a couple of them, asking who the sender was and what they wanted. He never got a reply to his questions, and eventually, they stopped, so he carried on as normal. Two weeks ago, as he was heading to his car at the end of a long day at the lab, he saw a folded white piece of paper tucked under the wipers on his windscreen.

Scribbled in thick black marker pen, the note read; **'I KNOW YOU LEFT THAT BOY FOR DEAD'**. His eyes darted around at the other cars in panic. He looked back at the building, but there was no one standing by the entrance and he was alone in the car park. His hand trembled as he opened the driver's door and as he was just about to climb into the driver's seat, a plastic bag was thrust over his head. He was marched across the car park and bundled into a small, red transit van. This was when he first met Ralf Harlow.

Ralf Harlow is a short, balding, overweight fifty-three-year-old Carpenter and struggling writer. He has self-published four mediocre crime novels, that never really took off. Ralf took a few creative writing courses and has always dreamed of making it big. Life hasn't really gone the way he planned, he is divorced, broke, and living at home with his elderly Mother - a consequence of gambling away his home and possessions three years ago. Earl does not know Ralf, but Ralf knows Earl. You see, the teenage boy that Earl left for dead, after stumbling upon him lying unconscious on the side of the road, was Ralf's nephew, Thomas.

Earl hadn't meant to leave Thomas to die, he had just been frightened. Earl had found him after he was run over, and the driver had vanished. In his panic, he thought anyone who arrived at the scene would think that *he* had attacked Thomas. As Thomas took his last, blood-gurgling breaths Earl had run away. On that dreadful day, Ralf had been driving home from work and noticed Earl standing over something on the ground. Ralf had pulled his van over and managed to get a good look at Earl's face before he left the scene. When Ralf got out of the van, expecting to see a dead animal, he crouched down and touched his nephew's cold skin. From that moment on, Ralf was hellbent on seeking justice for Thomas and making sure Earl got what he deserved.

Ralf has been watching Earl's career blossom for several years. He had been following Earl on social media. He read the congratulatory comments from Earl's loved ones when he graduated from University. He studied the photo of Earl shaking a professor's hand when he received an award for his PhD thesis. Ralf would park his van a few houses away from Earl's and watch him come and go. He had followed Earl to work for years and knew his daily routine like the back of his hand.

Initially, he was going to bribe Earl for a large sum of money to save his home, and, he had hoped, his marriage. But, one night, whilst he drank the best part of a bottle of whisky, and read another rejection email from a small publishing house, he had a better idea. He formulated a plan that required the Doctors' expertise.

Earl has something that Ralf needs - the ability to monitor and interpret brain waves. In the transit van, after Ralf kidnapped Earl, Ralf demanded he create a programme that would steal the ideas stored deep inside the brains of three bestselling authors. He has plans to write a super book, a book unlike any other, a book that will surely bring him fame. Ralf gave Earl two options – either he helps to steal the author's ideas and carries on living his life as normal without serving a prison sentence, or he can say no and be shot dead. Earl chose the first option.

Earl spent the past two weeks tweaking his MERKA (Measured Evaluation Recordings of Kinesthetic Activity) programme, which has only ever been used on mice, under the watchful eye of Ralf. Every evening, at 7.30 pm when the other staff have left for home, Earl swiped Ralf into the building, and Ralf pointed his gun as he watched Earl work. Earl doesn't know if the gun is even loaded, but he isn't going to take any chances. Ralf had turned up with a new 'subject' each night for the past three nights. Earl didn't know how he had kidnapped them, and he didn't dare ask.

There are three hospital beds in room 209. Above each bed is a whiteboard. Each whiteboard has a number written on it 1, 2, 3. Next to each of the beds is a machine, similar to one that you might see when somebody is on life support. Bed one contains a male, 49 years of age. He has penned 17 of the world's best-selling horror novels. Bed two contains a female, 26 years of age. She has published 12 thriller and suspense novels, one of which has been adapted into a film. Bed three contains a female, 64 years of age. She has written 25 best-selling science fiction novels.

The machine's wires are attached to each of the subject's temples with suction pads. The machines all beep out of sync, and dark green lines dart up and down the display screens. Each subject is unconscious, their brain waves being monitored and their dreams being collected and interpreted by Earl. When Earl has unpicked the subject's subconscious thoughts, he jots them down for Ralf to review. Earl hands Ralf the clipboard. "Here's yesterday's collection. Author No. 1 had a jewellery heist idea involving a main character with Aspergers. Author No. 2 had a prison escape idea involving corrupt prison guards. Author No. 3 had a virus that wipes out the entire male species idea."

"What's wrong with 1? His eyes are flickering and he's twitching" Ralf says, pointing his gun in the direction of Author No. 1's bed.

"He's waking up. I need to top up his propofol" Earl stutters.

"What are you waiting for then?" Ralf hisses.

Earl gulps, picks up an IV infusion set, and moves over to Author No. 1. He administers the potent, clear liquid into the IV drip. Thirty seconds later, Author No. 1 visibly relaxes. His arms stop twitching, and his eyes return to a fully closed position.

"He all good now?" Ralf asks with a raised eyebrow.

"Yes, I just need to monitor him for a while."

"Tell me more about No. 3's idea. She's had the best ideas so far" Ralf barks.

"She's got a beginning and an end. The middle isn't quite there yet. She's got an idea of freezing semen to keep reproducing after the world is torn apart by the deadly, mystery virus."

"Well start writing it down then!" Ralf repositions his gun to show that he isn't asking. He pulls a foil-wrapped ham salad sandwich out of his jacket pocket, takes a bite, and watches Author No. 1. He is fascinated by how all of this is working, he didn't think it actually would. In just a few more days, he should have enough material to start a first draft.

Earl starts scribbling away on his pad as he interprets the collected readings from Author No 3. He hopes that this collection will be enough and that the nightmare will soon be over. In the far right corner, in the third bed along, Author No. 3 opens her eyes. She moves her eyes to the right to look at both men. She has been awake for several hours and has been biding her time, waiting for the perfect moment to escape. She lifts her perfectly manicured right hand carefully and slowly so that she does not rustle the bed sheets. She carefully peels back the tape that is holding the cannula in place, and in one swift movement, she pulls the plastic tubing out and tucks the tube under the bed sheet next to her right leg.

Ralf stands up. "I need a slash. You are coming with me" he says. Earl stops writing and places his pen on top of the notepad. He walks rigidly toward the door with Ralf's gun pressed into the small of his back. When they have disappeared, Author No. 3 sits bolt-upright. She swings her navy legging-clad legs over the edge of the bed and frantically glances around the room, looking for something she can use as a weapon. She looks at the other two authors and recognises Author No. 1 from a book signing three years ago in NYC. She knows she should really help the other two, but there isn't any time. She scans the room quickly and notices that there's not much lying about that she can use as a weapon. She stands, but her legs feel like jelly and instantly give way. She drags herself across the floor, groaning with the effort it takes to pull her body away from the bed.

She glances up at the bedside table looking for her thick, black-framed glasses. She's blind without them. She can't see any of her personal belongings at all. No handbag, no phone, not even her boots. The only thing she can see, in that desperate search of room 209 is a white desk lamp, sitting on top of Earl's desk. She hauls herself forward to the edge of the desk and attempts to stand once more. She can hear Ralf and Earl's voices gradually getting nearer to room 209. She grabs the edge of the desk, levers herself up, stands as straight as she can, and pulls the desk lamp right out of the socket. She flicks her light grey hair out of her eyes, panting from the effort it took to grab the lamp.

They are right behind the door now. It's now or never. With all the inner strength she can muster she hauls herself towards the door just as Earl swipes the lock and opens it. She slams the lamp into Earl's temple.

He stares at Author No.3, dazed and surprised, then falls back against Ralf and his gun. Earl's key card drops to the floor. She grapples on the floor for the key card whilst Ralf pushes Earl off him. She picks it up and stands. Ralf doesn't know what to do. She shouldn't be awake. How is she awake? He aims his gun at her.

"Write my book or I will shoot you!" he screams. She swings the lamp at him. "I bet you couldn't even write a text, you sick bastard!" she croaks. On the floor, Earl is waking up. This is his moment, his chance to redeem himself, to right his wrongs after leaving Thomas to die. He runs at Ralf, pinning him against the wall. "Run!" he screams.

Author No.3 doesn't hesitate. Her bare feet thud along the cold flooring. She reaches the end of the corridor and turns left, finding the lift. As she waits for the doors to open she hears a gunshot. She presses the call button again and again, willing the doors to open. "Come on, come on!" she begs. The doors open, and she leans back against a large mirror panting as the lift descends. She gets out on the ground floor, hurries towards the exit, and swipes the keycard to open the turnstile by the reception desk.

She runs out to the car park, her feet screaming in pain as her soles crunch against the gravel. She's almost there now, she's almost free. She just needs to get onto the main road and flag down a car. She runs to the tall palisade perimeter fencing and freezes. The two gates that open out of the car park are bolted together with a thick steel chain and padlock, and the key is inside.

**

In a large Georgian townhouse, in Kensington, London, a woman sits typing on a brand new laptop on her shiny mahogany desk. Her office is positioned at the front of the house, and its large bay window lets in reams of beautiful, natural light. To the left of the desk, there are five rustic wood shelves neatly stacked with paperback and hardcover novels. On the desk, is a black and white photograph of the woman in her younger years, beaming at the camera as she clutches a paperback novel.

She takes her black, thick-rimmed glasses off, places them on the desk, and stretches her arms out in front of her. She interlocks her fingers, and pushes them out as far as she can, enjoying the satisfying click they make. She cricks her neck to the left, then the right, before pouring a large glass of champagne a ritual she has performed every time she finishes a novel. She renames the manuscript 'Author No.3', clicks save, and closes the laptop lid.

CHARLIE SPRATTEL

My name is Charlie Sprattel and this is my story. I was born on February 13th, 1976 at 3.35 AM at St Michael's General Hospital, in Selby, Yorkshire. My Mum, Gladys, a no-nonsense, down-to-earth Northern lass, used to tell anyone that would listen that I looked like an inside-out chicken in my first few hours, and she'd piss herself laughing at how her little Charlie Chuck piddled in Brian's (my Dad's) mouth, the first and only time he changed my nappy. Brian, my Dad, now gone, owned a chip shop on Ladybird Street. Mum and my aunt Diane, served on the counter, chain-smoking, gossiping, and knitting in between customers. Brian Sprattel was a tall, skinny bloke with a booming voice. He always wore a grey flat cap and twiddled the ends of his thick ginger Mustache whenever he told a white lie. When he wasn't busy slicing potatoes and battering fish, he would run out onto the cobbled road and have a kickabout with the local kids.

Gladys Sprattel, 4ft 11, with thick curly dark hair, a heaving bosom that gave her back problems, and a mouth the size of the Titanic, had done a typewriting course at college. She had planned to be a secretary, but a quick roll around with my father at her friend Beryl's birthday party resulted in the conception of my elder brother James, and that ended her secretary career before it even began. James was the clever one. As a kid, he wasn't interested in sports or girls. He had Mum's height and build, a mop of thick blonde hair, and blue eyes, and it was often joked that he was the 'milkman's.' He got all of his O Levels and went to University in London to study mathematics. He was hit by a car 10 years ago and died instantly. After his funeral, we found out he was gay. His partner of 5 years, attended the funeral and told Mum they were

10

in love. It did explain why he'd never liked sports or girls.

And me, well I was the opposite of our James. I didn't pass any exams. Not one. I did like the women though, oh yes. I liked boozing too, which was where it all began, and I suppose you could say, how I have ended up here. I got my Dad's build and features, and I certainly had a touch of the Northern charm. I was never short of a lass or two, even at the tender age of fourteen and usually had a pretty lass draping on my arm. I had an old head on my young shoulders, and folk used to joke that I was an old soul reincarnated in a boy's body. I couldn't do my sums, but I could write quite well and was always good at telling a story or two, and I could charm the pants off the local girls. It's a mix of the sweet and the sour, looking back at those times, when my life was simple, when life was good.

I got into some trouble when I was seventeen. I knocked about with the wrong crowd. I was jealous of our James and felt like since I was being treated like the black sheep of the family I might as well act like one. I started hanging about with Dean Whyte, the local hard knock. It started off in the usual way. A group of us would drink cheap cider in the park, smoke some fags, and flirt with lasses. It soon moved on to stealing from shops and getting chased by the owners. Somehow, I never got caught back then. One day, at the park, after a couple of hours of drinking some cheap cider, Dean pulled a little bag of white powder out of his pocket. His older brother had given it to him and said it was better than boozing, that it gives you an amazing buzz, and that you can shag for hours after taking it. His lass, Susan, was enjoying his increased stamina and his ability to talk for hours and have deep, meaningful conversations.

I suppose you can say, I was hooked from then on. It made me feel like I was immortal whenever I sniffed a line. It didn't take long for a full-blown habit to consume me, and I ended up getting sacked from my job at the factory. I was soon robbing more than just cigarettes and booze. I'm ashamed to admit it, but I robbed from my own Mum and Dad. I took the takings from the till one Friday night and spent it all on Cocaine. Dad gave me an ultimatum. Either I joined the army, and cleaned up my act or he would report me to the police. At the time I would have preferred the second option. I didn't have it in me to follow a regime or listen to orders. I couldn't even be arsed to get out of bed. But I could see how much I had upset them, and I wasn't wanted in the family home anymore.

So I enlisted with the Army Cadets in the Cairngorms, Scotland. I grew up – fast. Considering I never wanted to join, I ended up serving 18 years as a rifleman and toured Afghanistan. Mum and Dad were finally proud of their Charlie Chuck. For a few years, everything went well. I even met a nice lass, Mary, and we were together for five years. But, I still hadn't grown out of my womanizing ways, and I cocked it up didn't I? I can't blame her for ending it with me. I was still a pisshead. My army career came to an abrupt end when I stepped on an IED in Afghanistan and lost my right leg, and at the age of 34, I had to move back in with Mum and Dad.

The novelty of having their Charlie Chuck back at home with them soon wore off. I was a handful, and you have to remember they were getting on. The house had to be adapted for me to be able to get about in the wheelchair, and I was spending most nights screaming. Every time I heard a car backfire I would be back there, in Afghanistan, and I would lose my mind. Eventually, I was fitted with a prosthetic limb, and this helped me start getting out and about again. It also led me to start using stronger things than cocaine. That first time I smoked heroin the noise in my head stopped. Nothing mattered anymore. It didn't matter that I was disabled. It didn't matter that my parents were at their wit's end. It didn't matter that I wasn't working. Food didn't matter, women didn't matter, and all I needed in life was beer and heroin. I soon moved on to injecting, and I was back to robbing my folks to pay for the gear. One day, our Mum slapped me across the face and told me she wished I was dead. I told her I wished I was dead too. I left that day, and haven't seen her since. I didn't get an invite to our Dad's funeral.

I close the journal and put the biro in the front pocket of my faded black and white Nike rucksack. It's a cold, wet Manchester day. It's only 3 pm but it feels much later. I reposition my cardboard sign which reads 'Army vet, very hungry, please help.' The wind has blown it face down onto the soggy pavement. I put my other square piece of cardboard on the driest patch of pavement I can see, sit on it, put my plastic cup in front of my legs, and prop my back against a wall.

There's only £2.21 in it. It's been a slow day. I haven't eaten a thing since the half-chewed cheeseburger some pissed-up twat threw at me around 11 pm last night. I'm starving. If I go to the soup kitchen now, I will miss the afternoon rush to the train station. Most people are travelling home from school or work after 3.30 p.m, and that's the time of day when I'm most likely to get a few quid. So I will just have to stay hungry for now. I have got one can of super-strong cider left. I need to top up my earnings to buy some more. I open the can, take a swig, and place it on the floor. People rush past, heads down, busy texting on their phones. "Can you spare any change please?" I mutter as they walk past. They never even lift their heads, or make eye contact. I am pitied by these people. I am called 'tramp', 'hobo', and 'scrounger' every day. The truth is I pity *them*. Having money has made them ignorant.

They may have homes and salaries, but I see the most miserable, morally corrupt dregs of society pass by this train station. It is rare when a kind-hearted person stops to chat with me or gives me the time of day. Most of these people will never know what it is like to have to truly survive against all odds. I take another swig of cider and see Kelvin thundering towards me. I put my head down in panic. I owe him a tenner from the last score we had, and as usual, I had told him I was good for the money. I wasn't.

"No good putting your head down Charlie, I see you! Where's the money?" he shouts. He spits on the pavement before he reaches me, then throws his khaki green backpack next to mine. It knocks my full can over and I watch in horror as the yellow liquid trickles into the curb. I scramble to pick the can up, but he kicks it out into the road before I can grab it.

"That was my last can!" I stand up and we are face to face now. He grits his teeth and his gold tooth glints menacingly at me. His greasy, grey hair flops in front of one eye, and he pushes it out of the way with dirty fingernails.

"Dexter is going to be coming for blood now. You stupid bloody prick!" he throws a punch, but staggers and misses. He's half-cut and slurring his words. He falls into the wall and struggles to find his feet. He spins around and lunges for me again, this time he tries to head-butt me. I push him back and notice we have got an audience

14

now. There's a group of young lads filming on their phones, and people crossing the street to avoid us.

"Give me yer moneey" he slurs.

"I will get it to you for tomorrow, now do one Kelv, you're in no state for a scrap."

"Charlie Sprattel went to battle. Got blown up and now he's fucked. Poor old Charlie Sprattel" he sings.

He pushes me and I go flying into the path of a young woman with pink hair in pigtails. "Ow, watch it!" She groans. I hold my hands up in front of me. "I'm so sorry Miss. Are you alright?"

"Dickhead" Kelvin spits. He picks up his backpack and stumbles away towards the shopping centre.

"What was all that about?" the young woman asks with a raised eyebrow.

"I owe him some money. He's angry."

"I can see that. Here, take this."

She drops a £2 coin into my cup and repositions her bag on her shoulder. She has a kind face and I notice the lanyard around her neck with a photo ID of her smiling awkwardly in front of a white background. Her nails are painted bright orange, and she has tattoos all over one arm. She beams a bright smile at me and says "Have you had something to eat today?" I shake my head.

"I will be back in a minute," she says.

I watch her disappear into a coffee shop across the street. I try to guess her age, maybe thirty? I'm not used to people stopping for a chat and I start to feel a bit embarrassed. A few minutes later she jogs across the street holding two takeaway cups of coffee and a paper bag. "There you go," she says, as she hands me the coffee and a Danish pastry. I look back at her in surprise.

"Well eat it then! Or I will have it back" she laughs.

"Thank you," I say quietly.

"My name is Annie. And you are?

"Charlie. Charlie Sprattel."

"Have you got a place to stay Charlie?"

"No, I sleep here, usually."

I gratefully take a sip of the hot coffee, and in two large bites, the pastry is demolished. She stands watching me, and I ask myself why she is still here, why she is still talking to me.

"What do you do Miss?" I ask nodding my head at her badge.

"Homeless support worker. I was on my way home, but I have already missed the bus, so I have got a bit of time." She glances down at my things, and I see her looking at my journal.

"Are you a writer?" She asks without a hint of sarcasm like she is genuinely interested in me.

"No lass, these are just scribbles, thoughts, you know. Keeps me busy, I've got bugger all else to do." "Can I see?" She asks. I pick up the worn journal. The pages are curling up at the edges, the Green front cover is weather-worn, and I suddenly feel very self-conscious. She smiles as I hand it to her. She flicks through the pages, and then something piques her interest.

"These things really happened to you?" I nod and look down at the floor.

"This is really good Charlie. Have you ever tried to get it published?" I laugh with a loud roar. "Me, get something published? Don't be daft."

"Why not? I'm interested. I want to keep reading."

"Who is going to buy the scribbles of a homeless army vet?"

"I would. I will do you a deal. I walk past here at this time of day, Monday – Friday, week in and week out. We are going to formulate a plan. Get you off the streets, off the drugs, and onto the bookshelves."

I stare at her, wondering if *she* might be on drugs herself. She beams a bright smile at me. She's serious.

"Right, well I need to get off now, I'm starving, and I have got some chicken in the fridge that's about to go off. See you tomorrow." She gives a little wave and bounces off down the street like a huge ball of energy. I watch her for a bit, give a little shake of my head and smile. I return to the cardboard, finish my coffee and then open my journal, and start to write.

***

The morning passed slowly. I woke up in my sleeping bag dripping in sweat. I was rattling because I hadn't had a drink, or any heroin for two days. My entire body shook and there was a constant churning in my stomach. I slept fitfully. I don't remember my dreams, but I was feeling so uneasy, I knew they weren't pleasant. I mulled over my options. Kelvin would be coming back again for his money. I had checked my cup and saw a grand total of £5.46. I knew I was either going to have to give this to him and take the repercussions of it being short, steal from a shop, or steal someone's wallet. The third option was looking more and more likely.

I'd repositioned my cardboard, my cup, and my sign and sat watching the world go by. People with shopping bags, people rushing to work, people shouting angrily into their phones. The day has dragged, time moves very slowly when you haven't got anything to do. I don't want to be this person anymore. I am existing not living. I am crippled with fear every day, and the memory of being blown up comes like clockwork, every time I wake up, and every time I go to sleep. My brain is in constant fight mode, and the only thing that takes the edge of it is heroin. Annie's kindness yesterday has helped to remind me that there are some good people in the world, and she has seen the good in me. I have forgotten what good points I have.

I wonder if Annie will keep her word and show up. The afternoon rush has begun. I hold my cup out and ask for change. I get a few 5p and 2p coins thrown in. I roll a cigarette and sigh as I'm almost out of tobacco. The light is suddenly blocked by a figure standing over me. I look up and it's her.

"Hi, Charlie. Did you miss me?"

"I didn't think you would be back."

"If I make a promise I keep it. I've got some good news for you," she says with a grin.

"What kind of news?"

"I pulled a few strings last night. Someone owed me a favour. I'm taking you to see a room in shared accommodation. Come on get a move on or we will be late." I stare back at her.

"Come on then, the appointment is at four and it is a ten-minute walk."

"What do you mean a room, what kind of room? I haven't got any money?"

"I will tell you on the way."

I stand up and grab my backpack, then follow her. "Have you done any more writing?" She asks.

"A little yes. Look, Annie, I appreciate the trouble you have gone to, but no one is going to give me a room. I have no money for a deposit, no money for rent, and I am not on any benefits because I have no fixed address."

"I've already started your benefit forms. You need to sign them after, if you choose to take this room," She says. She lights a cigarette, inhales, and lets out a deep sigh. "Oh God, that's good. I needed that. It's been a pig of a day. Do you want one?"

I nod. "Thank you."

"There's one other thing I have done for you. I've made an appointment for you to get a methadone prescription. It's time to clean up your act, no excuses."

"I'm grateful for your help, honestly I am but why are you doing all this?" I ask.

"I've had my fair share of crap happen. I almost let it beat me. I suppose that's why I'm in the job I'm in now. To help others in a crisis," she says, as she flicks her cigarette.

"What happened?" I ask.

"Where do I start? My husband left me for a man. I couldn't afford to keep the house after he moved out. I developed a drinking problem and nearly lost my job. I couldn't get out of bed for about six weeks."

"Christ. Dreadful."

"Anyway, enough of that. We are here now," she says whilst pressing the doorbell.

I follow her in and stand sheepishly at the reception desk taking in my surroundings. The ground floor is an open space with grey carpeted floors and white walls. There is a reception desk and a smiley, overweight Jamaican man asks us to sign in. He chats with Annie for a while and throws his head back every so often cackling a deep throaty laugh. They obviously know each other well. I notice a staircase leading up to the bedrooms. There are plastic-framed pictures containing inspirational quotes such as 'Don't put off until tomorrow what you can do today.'

"Hi Charlie, I'm Ken. It's good to meet you. Shall we go and see the room?" the man at the desk asks. "Sure, thanks" I reply, and follow them both up the stairs. Ken opens the door and holds it for me so that I can walk in first. The room is spacious. The walls are painted a lemon colour, and the carpet is beige. There is a large window with white Venetian blinds, and a white plastic clock on the main wall. There is a wooden framed double bed, a pine wardrobe, and a pine chest of drawers. There is a matching pine desk in one corner of the room and a blue office chair. I notice another door to the right of the room and see a small ensuite with a shower cubicle, a toilet, a hand basin, and a small silver mirror. It's perfect. I gulp away my disappointment. I know I won't be able to afford it.

"What do you think?" Ken asks.

"It's great, but there's no way I can afford it."

"Well, you should thank your guardian angel Miss Annie here, as she's put the deposit down for you, and she's sorted the benefits out for you. All we need from you is a promise that you won't do any drugs here, and that you won't use antisocial behaviour. We have a zero-tolerance policy."

I turn to look at Annie. My mouth is wide open. "You'll catch flies in that gob if you aren't careful," she says.

"I can't accept this Annie. It's too much. I don't deserve it."

"I've got two conditions, Charlie. The first is, you need to stay off drugs. I will be coming to check on you and taking you to your appointments at the clinic. If you test positive for any drugs at all, you'll be out of here. The second is, I need to take a photocopy of your journal. I will give it back once I have, but I think it has the potential to be published."

I laugh and roll my eyes. "Are you kidding? Who's going to want to read a homeless bloke's journal?"

"Plenty of people, I reckon. If it is as good as Annie says it is, I will be reading it," Ken says, smiling.

"Right then, well let's get these forms signed," I say with a shrug. Annie throws her arms around me and squeezes me tightly. "Good choice. This is the start of your new life," she whispers into my ear. A large part of me is confused. Does Annie like me? I mean *fancy* me? I am attracted to her, but surely she doesn't fancy me…I am a state. She is beautiful, kind and funny. Why on earth would she be interested in a bum like me? I follow Annie and Ken down the stairs. I sign several pages of a contract, and benefit forms, not really understanding what I am signing, but just grateful to be given this chance. My head is whirring with excitement, anxiety, and confusion.

"See you in the morning Charlie. Bring your things around ten and we will get you moved in." Ken holds his hand out and I shake it firmly.

"I won't let you down," I say. I step out into the street. Annie lights a cigarette and holds one out for me. I shake my head, embarrassed by how much she has already done for me.

"What the hell just happened? Am I dreaming?" I say shaking my head.

"I've got a duvet and pillows I will bring over for you tomorrow. And a few bits like plates, mugs, cutlery, etc. Oh and before I forget here's my phone number." She hands me a folded piece of paper.

"I need your journal. I'm going to get it photocopied tonight. Is that Okay? I will bring it back tomorrow with the other bits?" I nod my head and pull the journal out of my backpack. I hand it to her, and she smiles at me.

"I'm really excited for you, Charlie. Big things are going to happen for you, I can sense it," she says. I smile back at her.

"You are absolutely incredible Annie. Do you know that?"

"Yep!" she says, laughing. There is a moment of awkwardness. I don't know whether to hug her again. Finally, she speaks.

"I will meet you here tomorrow at ten. Can you remember the way?"

"Yes. Annie, thank you" I say. I push a stray tear from my cheek. She winks at me, then turns and walks towards her bus stop.

***

Moving into my new room hadn't taken long at all, as I only had a rucksack with a few clothes and my sleeping bag. Annie had met me on the day I moved in, with a few extra bits to make it homely. She had bought me a peace lily houseplant in a bright blue pot. I've kept the plant alive for 94 days. I've also been clean and sober for 96 days. I am still on methadone but they have reduced the dose. Hopefully, in a couple of weeks, I will be off it altogether.

On the whole, life has been going great. I have kept my head down, and I have even got a little part-time job at the Greggs a few doors down from the house. There has been one shitty moment, though. One of the other residents broke into my room last month and stole the small, second-hand TV and PlayStation I had saved really hard for. I had a wobble, and in my anger, I went out to score. I didn't use though. Every fibre of my being wanted to, but I stopped myself before I reached the corner of the street where Dexter deals from. I returned to my room, wrote for a bit, calmed down, then called Annie.

I still have flashbacks from when I was blown up, they will never go away, but I have learned to manage them better. I have recently started Cognitive Behavioural Therapy and it is helping me process everything that has happened. I have even spoken to my Mum, and later this evening, I am getting the train up to see her. I'm dead nervous. We have a lot of work to do if we want to repair our *relationship. I can't describe how good it feels though, to know she wants to see me.*

I put my pen on the desk, and glance up at the clock. It's time. Ken knocks on my door three times. I open it and he stands at the doorway, beaming his big toothy grin.

"You ready?" he asks.

"I'm ready."

We walk down the stairs and into the communal room on the ground floor. The host extends his hand, and I shake it. I stare at the camera, the microphone, and a young, ginger lad and a slim, blonde woman, who are busy setting up. I am suddenly flooded with anxiety, and my hands start to shake.

"Try not to be too nervous Charlie. We can do a few takes until we get it right, there's no rush," the presenter says as he limply shakes my hand. He nods towards the two seats laid out in the centre of the room. I take a seat and clear my throat.

"We all ready?" the host asks. I look around and see the ginger lad behind the camera, and the blonde woman holding a large microphone, standing next to a large ring light.

"Ready when you are," the ginger lad says.

The host nods at me, I gulp and nod back.

"My name's Dan Jefferson, from Look North, and I am joined today by a very special guest, Charlie Sprattel. You might have already heard Charlie's name before, as his memoir – I Am Charlie, has recently been published and is now available to buy in bookstores and online. Charlie, how does it feel, to know people are buying and reading your book?"

"It doesn't feel real Dan, to tell you the truth. The last couple of months have been unbelievable really. I never dreamed anyone would want to read about my life."

"You were in the army, and you lost your leg in

Afghanistan, correct?"

"Yes, that's right. I ended up on the streets a few months later. I battled with drug and alcohol addiction, but I'm clean and sober now. Writing helped me cope. And Annie, the most incredible woman I have ever met."

I continue answering Dan's questions, but in the corner of my eye, I can see her pink hair poking around the door frame. She's watching me. I turn to look at her and she puffs out her cheeks and squashes them with both hands, then throws her head back laughing. I cough to cover my laugh, then resume my 'serious' face for the rest of the interview. When the interview is over, and I have thanked Dan and his crew and said my goodbyes, she breezes over.

"Well, that went well! Can I have your autograph?" I roll my eyes at her. She sits on my lap and puts her arm around my neck.

"The question is, are *you* nervous?" I ask her.

"A little bit, what if she doesn't like me?" she asks, looking down at the floor.

"She will love you. Just as much as I do."

We kiss for a few minutes. Time stops and I relish the feeling. Warmth, joy, happiness and hope.

"Come on then, Charlie Chuck, let's get that train." We walk toward the train station hand in hand. I've been given a second chance in life, and I am going to make every second count.

The Overnight Success

John likes to write late at night, that's just the way it is. He needs silence. He needs to hear his thoughts, his fears, and his desires. Sometimes he just sits and listens to the sounds of the night. Rain, wind, a fox rummaging through a bin bag, and black cabs unloading drunken Millennials. He had been lucky with his first novel. He hadn't actually believed it was any good but published it anyway. To his amazement, it sold 100,000 copies in three months. The press gave him the nickname 'The Overnight Success' and it has stuck to him like shit ever since.

He has written several of his best sellers at night. He can find inspiration in anything. Correction, he *used* to be able to find inspiration in anything. Most days he struggles with writer's block. On a good day, he might be able to write 500 words. He usually ends up throwing them away, the words just aren't good enough. He feels like a fraud. He is getting old, and he just doesn't have anything worthwhile to say anymore.

People have high expectations for his next novel. His most recent novel *Choose* has been adapted into a box-office hit movie. Tanned and toned, talentless actors play his mediocre characters. He hates the film. He has managed to write four chapters of his new novel, that's all. His hands are sweaty as he sits staring at the one sentence he has typed in chapter five. He's deleted the sentence over and over and over again, then retyped the same sentence because he can't think of anything better.

He knows what the problem is. He's feeling unbelievably guilty and he can't shake the feeling off. It is all to do with money, he has too much of it. Stupid amounts of money. He doesn't deserve it. He's not a good writer, he's just been lucky. He used to write for fun. Now he has to write to keep his agent happy. He has to satisfy his fans. He wants out. This novel will be the last thing he ever writes if he ever manages to complete it.

Of course, his wife Karen won't let him give up writing. Money, holidays, material things – they all matter to her. He smirks as he thinks about the woman he met twenty years ago. That woman couldn't get enough of him. She would beg him to take her on the back seat of her Mother's car. She would run from taxis to avoid paying. She used to dance laughing in the rain. That woman was long gone. He's scared their kids will change too. Danny is too young to understand fame and greed, but Molly, well Molly is becoming more and more like her Mother every day.

Whenever he gets writer's block he logs onto the message forum on his website and reads the latest comments and reviews. One fan in particular, *Blogger666* he calls himself seems to be obsessed with John's novels. This bloke regularly posts messages to other fans, 'In *Choose* which way would you prefer to die?' or comments like 'just watched *Choose* for the third time today, I love the bit where Catherine gets beheaded, I'd love to rub her blood all over myself.' John is thankful that he'll never have to meet the sick bastard.

He is thinking about calling it a night, he sighs at the thought of getting into bed with Karen. He doesn't love her anymore and he knows she doesn't love him. She loves his money though, he's certain of that. He's stayed up late every night for the past month just to get away from her. Sometimes he masturbates in the indoor swimming pool whilst he thinks about the young blonde across the street with a perfect round arse and big breasts. He hadn't even wanted the pool, they live in London not LA.

He is fed up with keeping up appearances. He just wants a normal, quiet life. Karen had gone on at him for months about how much she wanted a pool, and how she was embarrassed that she was the only one in her group of friends that didn't have one. The ungrateful cow has only used the pool a handful of times. She's now bored of it and wants a gym instead.

It's been raining hard all night. He pours a Jack Daniels and stands watching the rain through the kitchen window. He's waiting for inspiration to strike. Nothing. He pours another Jack and turns his back to the window. Oreo, his fat black and white cat, walks across the window ledge. Her loud Meow shocks him and he drops his glass. "Stupid Cat!" he curses as he kneels down and begins to pick up pieces of broken glass from the white marble floor. He can hear a faint tapping at the front door. He isn't sure if he is imagining it, or if it's just the wind knocking the hanging basket against the porch window.

He sighs as he begins turning off the lights. It's time to climb the stairs and get into bed with the miserable bitch again. As he reaches the third step up, he hears the tapping again. He walks back down, turns on the lights, and looks through the window pane of the large, heavy oak door. He can't see anything there, but he can still hear the tapping. It's really starting to mess with his head. He pushes his feet into his slippers, opens the door, and steps outside into the rain. A furious gust of wind slams the door shut. The hanging basket sways vigorously back and forth, he takes the basket off the bracket and puts it on the floor. Dirt spills out from the basket all over his slippers. He crouches down and starts pushing the dirt off his feet.

He looks up and sees a tall, sturdy figure emerging from the shadows. He moves closer and stands at the end of John's immaculate white gravel drive.

"Hello?" he calls out to the stranger.

The stranger starts to move across the driveway. There's something over the stranger's face. The mask is grotesque and appears to be made from pig skin. The stranger reaches inside his jacket pocket as he gets closer to the door. John stumbles back fumbling with the door handle. "Get off my drive! This is private property, I'm calling the police!" he stammers. He feels the door swing open and backs into the porch. He fumbles with the lock, trying to get it to catch. The stranger presses his pig mask against the glass window pane and taps the Oak door lightly with his clenched fist.

"I'm calling the police!" he shouts. He searches in his pocket for his mobile phone. "Where's my phone, where is it!" he shrieks. He runs up the stairs and opens his bedroom door. He shakes Karen's shoulders. "Wake up Karen!" he says.

She sits up, confused and unable to see anything in the pitch-black room. "What's going on? What time is it?" she croaks.

"Shush. Keep your voice down."

"What the hell's going on?"

"There's someone trying to get in the house. Get the kids and go to the utility room and lock yourselves in there."

"Have you called the police?" she asks.

"I can't find my phone."

She reaches across the glass-top bedside table for her phone. "Oh my God. The kids!" She shrieks.

"I need you to be brave Karen. Do you understand? Get the kids. Go!"

She creeps across the plush grey carpeted landing towards Danny's bedroom. Gently, she scoops Danny into her arms and fumbles through the dark. She inches towards Molly's room, trying to avoid the one creaky floorboard she knows is there, somewhere. She carefully opens Molly's door. She gently shakes her daughter's shoulders. "Molly. Molly, wake up."

"Mum?"

"Listen, you need to be quiet. Someone's trying to get in the house. We need to go downstairs, come on quickly." Karen leads the way, clutching Danny against her breast. Molly follows with heaving breaths. They tip-toe down the stairs. The sound of shattering glass makes Molly lose her footing. Molly grabs at the banister to steady herself.

"Run!" Karen screams.

They sprint for the utility room. Baby Danny flings his head back and starts to wail. Karen squints as she looks around the dark, utility room looking for a safe place to hide the children. She places Danny in a laundry basket and covers him with a towel. There is nowhere for Molly to hide. At fourteen she is too tall to fit into the cupboards she used to hide in a few years ago. Karen wheels the tumble dryer across the black tiled floor and pushes it against the back of the door. She glances around for other heavy items that she can stack against the door. He's not getting to her kids, no way. "He better have called the police already," she mutters.

John moves across the cool walls of his study, desperately searching for the light switch. He can hear the stranger breathing. The stranger's raspy breaths compete with the thud, thud, thud of John's heartbeat. Finally, his fingertips find the switch. He squints as his eyes adjust to the light. He can't move, fear runs through him like a gust of freezing cold air as he stares at the pig-man in the bright yellow glow. He cowers in disbelief as the stranger snorts like a pig over and over again.

"Stop it! Stop it! Stop it!" he screams, pressing his hands firmly against his ears. Adrenaline kicks in when he remembers the children are in the utility room. He runs for his writing desk knowing that a pen knife is buried somewhere deep inside. He pulls the drawer from the desk and tips the contents out. Pens and post-it notes and half-finished manuscripts scatter the porcelain floor. "Just take what you want and leave us alone!" John screams, then throws himself at the cordless phone on his desk. The stranger lunges forward and rips the phone's base from the socket.

"I have money. Lots of money. I'll open the safe. You can take what you want. If you go now, I promise I won't tell a soul" John begs as he backs away. The stranger throws himself at John and grabs him by the throat. He feels his rancid, hot breath in his ear.

"I want to watch you kill your wife" the stranger whispers.

"No. I won't. I can't. You're sick, you need help. I can get you some help" John splutters. The stranger pulls a shiny, thick knife from the inside of his long black coat. He pushes up John's Merino wool sleeve and slices the knife across his forearm. John wails in agony, his blood drips onto the floor like crimson raindrops.

"If you don't do it, I will murder your children while you watch. Then I will kill you." The stranger's deep, demonic voice entices the small hairs on John's arms to stand to attention. John shakes his head and heaves at the thought of butchering Karen. Vomit flows across the porcelain in hot, rancid waves. The stranger grabs John by the arm and drags him along the hall. "Remember to do as I say and the children will be fine" the stranger barks.

John leans his head against the utility door. He tries the handle.

"It's me he's gone. I scared him off" he says.

"Where's the police?" Karen screams.

"I called. They are coming. I caught him trying to steal from my desk drawer. He ran when I put the study light on." His heart pounds as he waits for her to open the door. He listens to the sound of the tumble dryer's wheels squeaking across the tiled floor, then takes a deep breath as the door opens.

"You're bleeding! What happened?" She shrieks.

"I caught my arm on some broken glass. He knocked the lamp over when he was rummaging through the drawer."

"Was he after money?" She asks.

"He might have been looking for my new manuscript."

Karen swallows. There's something different about him. After twenty years with the man, she knows when he's lying. His empty, dark eyes stare right through her. "Dad, what's wrong?" Molly whispers.

"We need to put the children back to bed, I don't want them down here when the police arrive," Karen says as she picks Danny up from the basket.

"Put him down" John hisses.

"He needs to go to bed!"

"I said put him down" John shouts.

"You're scaring me" Karen shrieks.

John grabs his wife by the hair and pulls her out of the room.

"Dad! Stop!" Molly screams.

"Stay here. Look after Danny. Close the door" Karen calls behind her.

Molly clambers to the door, closes it, and sobs silently. Karen slaps at John's arms as he pulls her along, trying to get free from his grip. "GET OFF ME!" She sobs. He throws her across the tiles in the study. "Why are you doing this? Why?" She whimpers. She gulps as she notices a pool of blood by his desk. Next to the pool of blood is a crimson-stained pen knife, surrounded by opaque pieces of broken glass.

He pins Karen against the tiles, his body weight pressed on top of her. He turns to look at the stranger standing by the door. The stranger lifts up his mask and John sees the stranger's identity for the very first time. He looks at the familiar face. A smile spreads across his face as he wraps Karen's hair around his knuckles and pulls. He snorts and grunts, and bites her shoulder.

"Stop, please, stop" Karen begs.

"He told me to. He'll kill the children if I don't. Look, he's watching, he's nodding in approval."

"There's no one here!" She screams.

She reaches her hand across the tiles, struggling under his weight trying to grab the edge of the pen knife. "I hate you! Money, money, money, that's all you've ever wanted. What about me? What about what I want, huh?"

Karen twists her face against the smooth cold tiles to avoid his deadly stare. "This isn't real, it's just a dream" she chants. John pulls at her face and twists it back to look at him. He runs his fingers across his injured arm and smears blood across Karen's lips before kissing her roughly. He thrusts the penknife into her throat, over and over again until he feels her body go limp. He stares up at the ceiling, panting with exhaustion. A few seconds later his heart starts to slow. Adrenaline starts to drip away, and there's a churning deep in his gut. He looks down at Karen's blood-drenched lifeless body. He stumbles back staring at the blood covering his hands. "What have I done? Oh God, What have I done?" he whimpers. He catches sight of his reflection in a huge, lavish silver mirror. The tall, sturdy frame is his, but the menacing face that stares back at him belongs to someone else.

He turns to face Karen's body. He knows what he has to do. It's the only way he can stop the visions and the voices. He has to stop himself before he hurts the children. He runs the knife across his wrists and lies next to Karen for the very last time.

THE WISHING
TREE

Brown, yellow, and orange leaves crunch underneath the soles of her trainers. The sun is about to set. She chose this time of day, to hang herself, as she wanted to see one more beautiful sunset. She doesn't feel sad, or scared, just relieved. The time is right. All of her affairs are in order and four handwritten notes in envelopes are stacked neatly on the freshly polished dining room table.

She heads for the large oak tree in the middle of the woods. Many people have successfully hung from it in the past, so she is sure it will get the job done. She puts her bag at the foot of the tree, unzips it, and pulls out the rope. The evening sun picks up the auburn tones of her long, curly hair. It is beautiful, shiny, and glowing. It is ironic, the vibrancy of her hair, and the dewy glow of her skin, considering how dead she feels inside. She inhales a deep breath of humid air. It has been an unusually warm October. A rustling sound startles her. She spins her head in the direction of the trees behind her and watches a grey squirrel scurrying about in the leaves.

The squirrel stops and gives her a knowing look, then darts off across the woodland. In the clearing, she notices a tree with colourful ribbons tied around the heartwood. She hadn't noticed it before. She throws the rope on the ground and walks over to take a closer look. She pulls at a green ribbon on the tree. '**Please make my Dad better. Please let him live'** is written in faded black marker pen. She reads from a white ribbon **'God please answer my prayers.'**

There is a weather-worn, wooden box beside the tree. The lid creaks as she opens it. Inside there are purple, red, orange, and yellow ribbons and a black marker pen. She picks a yellow ribbon, and leans on the lid of the box to write '**I wish I was someone else.'** She ties the ribbon to the tree, then heads back to the Oak tree to finish what she'd started. Her emerald green eyes are clouded with tears. She shakes her head furiously, this is not the time to be consumed with emotion.

When she reaches the Oak tree she is stunned to see that the rope and her bag are gone. She spins around, frightened that she's not alone. Her ears prick at every single sound - a gentle breeze rustling through the trees, the sound of leaves falling to the ground, the old woodland breathing at the end of a warm day.

"Hello?" she calls out.

Only the birds reply. A jay shrieks in annoyance and a woodpecker frantically pecks at a tree, the incessant pecking matches the rhythm of her rapid heartbeat.

She walks deeper into the woods, confused and frightened. The sun has almost disappeared and darkness looms. She should be dead now. She needs to find the rope. In the distance, she sees a small doorway, surrounded by large, grey, square stones and rocks.

"What the hell?" she says out loud. She has been to these woods at least fifty times before. She used to walk Max here, with Scott, when they were happy and life was full of promise and plans for the future. A tear escapes as she remembers the time she slipped in the mud, trying to throw a stick for Max. Scott could hardly breathe, he was laughing so hard at the mud caked on her leggings and hands. Scott died six months ago, but it still feels like yesterday to Ruby. She can't and won't live without him.

The door is tiny, almost child-size. There is a round brass knob in the centre. She rubs her eyes, convinced that she's in the midst of a dream, and any moment now she will wake up in her dark bedroom, shrouded by that familiar thick veil of grief. She places a hand on the knob and turns it clockwise. The door creaks open. She steps forward, and peers in cautiously. A dimly lit, winding tunnel is laid out ahead of her.

There are candle lanterns hanging on each side of the tunnel's walls. She lowers her head and steps in. The door slams behind her. She spins around and pulls at the handle. It doesn't budge. "No, no, no, no!" she shouts. She can hear the hollow sound of bongo drums in the distance. '*What the hell have I walked into?*' she thinks to herself. She walks toward the sound of the drums and hears footsteps approaching.

"Don't be frightened, Elmara" a female voice whispers in the shadows.

"Who's there?" She stutters.

"We've waited for you for such a very long time," a male voice says.

"Stay back, don't come any closer!" she shrieks. The footsteps get louder, and the strangers get closer. She turns for the door, and to her horror it has disappeared. All that remains is a solid, stone wall. They are behind her now. She feels their eyes burning into the back of her head. She turns slowly, her eyes wide as she looks at the man and woman in front of her.

"I am Oedine and this is Noros. We are so glad you are here, Elmara," the woman says. She has long white hair that flows across her delicate shoulders. Her floor-length white dress is gathered at the waist with a rope belt, and there is a gold P brooch nestled in the fabric around her collarbone. Her azure eyes are ethereal, and her ivory skin glows in the dim light. Noros is tall and muscular. An orange cloak drapes across his flawless black skin, and his braided hair emphasises his prominent jawline.

"My name is Ruby! Where has the door gone? Let me out!"

"Come with us, we need to show you something," Noros says, gesturing towards the tunnel.

"I don't belong here. Whatever this is, whoever you are, I'm not meant to be here. Let me out."

"That world out there, it isn't real" Oedine sighs. "It felt pretty real this morning when I was…" Ruby stops, unable to finish the sentence, unable to say 'When

I was buying rope to kill myself.'

"You are the chosen one, Elmara, it will all make sense soon. You'll see. Trust us," Noro says. He clicks his fingers, and a second later the three of them are out of the tunnel. Ruby blinks as her eyes adjust to the bright light. She shakes her head. "Right what the hell was that? Did you just make us teleport? I need to wake up now." she says. Oedine pinches the skin under Ruby's arm. "Ow!" Ruby hisses. "Would you have felt that if you were asleep?" Oedine asks.

Ruby gazes around at her surroundings. There are several white tents positioned in a large circle. She watches as a woman dressed in a beige linen dress adds a log to a burning fire. On the other side of the camp, an elderly woman taps away at the bongo drums, and a young man with a shaved head plays a melody on a violin. There are young children weaving in and out of the tents, laughing. A young girl, with white blonde plaited hair and piercing blue eyes, walks over to Ruby and gestures to her to lower her head. She places a handmade floral headdress delicately on Ruby's auburn curls. "What is this place?" Ruby asks.

"This is the ancient land of Phosphiet. Elmara, you are in another realm, the world you have come from is not where you belong," Oedine says soothingly.

"There is only one world, this isn't real."

"Let me ask you this Elmara, were you happy in your other life? You came to the woods to end your life didn't you?" Noros asks raising an eyebrow.

"I wasn't happy no, but I don't belong here. I'm not the person you are looking for," Ruby replies.

"Walk with me," Oedine says. Ruby follows Oedine and Noros through a lush green field adorned with the brightest purple bluebells she has ever seen. Everything in Phospiet seems to glow. Colours are vivid, the people are beautiful, the people are *happy.*

"Our World is on the brink of extinction. There is

only one person who can save us all, and that's you," Oedine purrs.

"And how am I supposed to save you?" Ruby asks.

"Every thirty years we must make an offering to the Gods. The Gods choose who they want. We do not. We have no control over who is chosen. We do not decide if the offering is male or female, a child or an adult. The Gods send the chosen one when the time is right, and it is our duty to play our part in the prophecy," Oedine says firmly.

Ruby notices a sudden change in the atmosphere. Oedine is no longer soothing and reassuring. Her azure eyes are cold and dark, her lips twisted into a smirk. Noros begins to close in on Ruby.

"Offering? What do you mean, offering?"

Ruby backs away from them, and trips, falling into the grass. Behind her, she hears the people of the camp stampeding over the field. They are chanting as they run 'Phospiet, Phospiet, Phospiet, Phospiet!'

"The Gods require your blood Elmara. You are Elmara the Brave. They have been watching you since you were born. They have seen you overcome many battles," Noros says.

"My name is Ruby!"

The people of the camp make a circle around her. There is nowhere to run. They link hands, and continue chanting 'Phosphiet, Phosphiet, Phosphiet, Phosphiet.'

"Please stop this, I want to go home. Please!" she cries.

"Oh powerful Gods, hear our words. Elmara the Brave is home, she is your chosen vessel. Take her blood, and may Phospiet ever prosper!" Oedine shouts. The circle begins to close in and Ruby watches in horror as they begin to pull blades from pouches around their waists. Even the children are wielding knives.

Ruby tilts her head towards the sky and roars. Her

assailants hold their hands to their ears and recoil in agony. There's something in the pitch of her scream that seems to be causing them pain. Oedine and Noros fall to their knees. Ruby starts to run.

"Chase her Noros, quickly!" Oedine screams. Noros tries to stand up but he can't. His knees buckle, and he bends over the grass clutching his head. Ruby runs past the tents. "Shit, shit, shit! I want to live, I want to live! She screams. As soon as the words leave her lips she sees the portal open up. The door appears and swings wide open and the dimly lit, winding tunnel is in sight. A magnificent, gravity-defying force pulls her body towards the door, sucking her through the entrance, and pushing her along the tunnel. It happens so quickly she has no time to think, or process what's happening, she is just relieved to be away from Phosphiet and its cult of crazies.

***

"Over here, we are over here!" a middle-aged, bearded man shouts, whilst giving a wave of his hand. "Calm down Rex," he says to his French Bulldog who is barking furiously. The paramedics run across the woodland, struggling with the weight of their equipment.

"Thank God you are here! It was me who called you. I was walking Rex and I found her like this."

The female paramedic crouches down and starts to check Ruby's airways and feels for a pulse.

"She's alive," she says to her male colleague. She pulls the snapped noose from Ruby's neck and her male colleague places an oxygen mask over Ruby's mouth.

"Has she said anything to you at all?" the paramedic asks the dog walker.

"No. I thought she was dead. I only found her because Rex ran over here and was barking at something. I thought he was chasing a squirrel or something, you know? It's absolutely dreadful, poor woman," he shakes his head.

"Hello, can you hear me? My name is Jenny and I'm a paramedic. If you can hear me open your eyes." Ruby's eyes flicker. She moves her head to the side and lifts a hand to pull the oxygen mask off her face.

"No lovely, you need to keep that mask on, it's to help you breathe," the male paramedic says. Ruby slowly opens her eyes and stares at the paramedics. She is trying to say something.

"We need to get her in the ambulance," Jenny says. The paramedics carefully load her onto the gurney. They thank the dog walker for his help, then head for the ambulance.

Jenny sits in the ambulance with Ruby. "Ready to go when you are Malc," she says. Malcolm activates the sirens and they head for the hospital. "There's no purse or phone or anything in her bag, Malc," Jenny says.

"What's your name my love?" Jenny asks leaning over, gently lifting the oxygen mask.

"Elmara. My name is Elmara."

The Anger Issue

"You're listening to New Forest Xtra FM, I'm your host Dane Ellis, and it's that time of night people.. it is time for 'The Anger Issue.' We've got callers on the line ready to tell us what really gets their goat. What makes you angry? Text us on 80028 or message us on our Facebook page."

Dane turns down the mic, and plays 'Mr Brightside.' "Who's first up to speak?" he asks the producer, Steve. "Roger from Milford on Sea. He's got a stutter, so go easy on him." Steve's assistant Mae, puts her hand to her mouth to cover a giggle. Steve flashes her a wide grin.

"Ha! Ssssssure will," Dane replies. Steve shakes his head and takes a sip of coffee. Dane winks at Steve, runs a hand through his shoulder-length brown hair then fades down the music.

"We are joined by Roger from Milford on Sea. Hi Roger, tell me, what is it that really gets you angry?" "Bin men. They are bloody u u u u useless. I've complained to the council no end of times. They can't even be arsed to put the bins back at the right house. My bin has got b b b b bright yellow flower stickers on it and a big fat 71 on it, and they still put it outside Doreen's at number 79!"

"Ah Roger what a nightmare! You've even personalised your bin! How can they get it so wrong?" Dane rolls his eyes at Steve mouthing the word 'Gimp.' Steve laughs quietly, his fat shoulders shaking with the effort it takes to stay composed.

"Ye Ye Yes, it makes me wonder what we pay our council tax for really," Roger continues.

"Have you ever called the council to complain?" Dane asks.

"Fat lot that would do. They aren't interested. D D D Doreen is at her wits end!"

"Oh Gosh, well Roger pass on my regards to Doreen and I hope the bin men get their act together soon! Take care mate, and thanks for calling New Forest Xtra FM." Steve holds up a piece of paper 'MARTIN FROM MINSTEAD.'

"Hello Martin, are you having bin problems too?" Dane asks leaning into the microphone. "Hello Dane, erm no, it's inconsiderate drivers that really piss me off!"

"Martin, I have to remind you that we are live on air, no swearing please."

"Sorry, forgot myself there. I get angry when people park across the pavement not leaving enough room for wheelchair users or people with pushchairs," Martin grumbles.

"Ah Martin, I'm with you on that one. Really annoying that is," Dane says sarcastically. He puts a hand to his mouth and mimics a yawn.

"Well, I'm a wheelchair user you see, and it is dangerous going around parked vans."

"It sure is buddy. So New Forest XTRA FM listeners, if you are someone who parks inappropriately, think of Martin in the future and the danger you are putting him in. Give me a song Martin before you go. We will be taking more calls in a few minutes."

"Oh, erm, I can't think. Erm. Okay, I've got one. Peter Gabriel, Solsbury Hill, thanks, Dane."

"Good choice Martin. Have a nice evening mate." Dane fades down the mic and plays the song. "Jesus Christ, they are a right bunch of boring sods tonight Steve!" Dane takes a swig from his coffee. "What we got next? Parking fines? Price of butter? Which to be honest, is actually shocking at the moment."

"And the price of ketchup!" Mae adds. Colour floods to her cheeks as soon as the words leave her lips. She is still new to the role, and always feels nervous when she contributes to discussions with Steve and Dane. Dane has never been horrible to her, but at times she has felt like a hindrance rather than being helpful. He is experienced and a good presenter, and she admires him, but he never really speaks to her unless Steve is involved in the conversation.

"I think you'll like this next one. His name is Elliott and he's been taking those herbal happy pills the Yanks love. You've probably seen the adverts for them on TV recently. The pills help with depression and anger. Apparently, they aren't antidepressants or anything like that. He reckons they've made him much happier," Steve says.

"Oh yeah, those 'Happy You' pills? Are they NHS or FDA approved?" Dane asks.

"I dunno…" Steve replies.

"How the hell are you still the producer here, you're absolutely shocking at your job mate."

"Ah come on, you know I had a heavy one last night." Steve replies.

"What's your excuse for all the other shows then? You weren't hungover when we had the crazy cat ladies section last week. That was a bloody disaster!" Steve shrugs, as the song comes to an end. Dane moves in front of the mic. "Great song that, love it. Right XTRA FM listeners, prepare yourselves as this next caller has something really interesting to tell us. Elliott, how are you doing tonight?"

"Hello, Dane! I am very well thank you, very well indeed!"

"Yes! Loving the energy there Elliott. Come on then, what's your secret? Why are you so happy, this is a section on what makes people angry ha-ha!"

"Well Dane, two months ago I was researching alternatives to antidepressants. I used to have depression you see. I wasn't just depressed, I was angry all the time. I was snapping at my kids, I got into quite a few rows at work. I was just really unhappy. Anyway, I was prescribed antidepressants. And they were just dreadful. I felt like a robot. I couldn't show any emotion, it didn't matter if I was happy or sad, I would just be expressionless."

"It's a common problem isn't it, with antidepressants, or so I'm told," Dane says.

"It is. And I didn't want to be dependent on tablets for the next God knows how many years, so I started looking at alternatives. And there was the usual stuff, you know, go for a nice walk, do yoga, meditate, and so on, and well I had tried all those things," Elliott says.

"So what did you end up doing?" Dane asks.

"I saw an advert for a company called 'Happy You' online. At first, I thought it was some kind of dieting company, but the banner grabbed my eye. It said 'Millions of happy customers. Natural ingredients – zero chance of dependency.'

"Sounds a bit of a gimmick to me, to be honest mate, they are that American company with the goofy advert of people on roller skates aren't they?" Dane asks.

"They are an American company, yes, but hear me out. I spent days researching them, reading reviews, watching YouTube videos, you name it I did it."

"So how do these natural ingredients 'happy pills' help so many people then? And how have they helped you?"

"I don't know how to explain it really, they've just given me a zest for life again. My marriage is better, I'm happier, so my wife is happier, the kids are happy that their Dad has the energy to play with them again, and I'm smashing it at work lately. I'm even getting on with my mother-in-law!" Elliott says.

"Well getting along with the mother-in-law is a reason to try them, isn't it fellas? Producer Steve, Google the link right away!" Dane laughs. "What are the ingredients in these magic tablets?"

"St John's Wort, Chamomile, and a few other things that I can't remember off the top of my head. Most of my work colleagues are taking them now. Some of these blokes, and they won't mind me saying this, used to get into scraps on a Friday night down the local pub, and now they are helping old ladies pack their shopping in supermarkets or volunteering at soup kitchens."

"Well, they certainly sound interesting Elliott. Do you work for the company?" Dane snorts.

"No, I work in Construction. They've saved my life, they really have."

"So is there a big following, here in the New Forest?" Dane asks, his interest waning as he signals to Steve that it's time to wrap up the call. There is silence on the line. "Elliott, are you still there mate?" There is no response. Dane and Steve exchange glances and Steve looks down at his watch. Mae straightens in her chair.

"I think we might have lost Elliott there folks. Elliott, are you with us?" Elliott's breathing is heavy. He is still on the line, but he doesn't speak. Dane is about to pull the plug on him, thinking that he's one of those heavy-breather pervert types when a woman suddenly screams 'Oh my God Elliott what is happening to you?!' Dane looks over at Steve, his skin is ashen and his eyes are wide with panic. "What do we do?" he mouths silently. "Elliott, is someone there with you? What's happening, are you safe?" he asks. "He's frothing at the mouth and his eyes are bleeding! Send an ambulance, please, quickly, Oh God!" the female voice shrieks. "Hello, who is speaking?" Dane asks.

"I'm Elliott's wife, Michelle. Something is happening to him, I think he is having some kind of seizure! No, Elliott, stop, get off me. Ow! You are hurting me!" The line goes dead, and there is a stunned silence in the studio. Dane has never experienced anything like this before and he doesn't know what to do. He sits rooted to the spot, staring blankly into space. Steve lowers his head and gulps. There are beads of sweat pooling around his temples. He looks at his screen and he can see that calls are pouring in from concerned listeners. "Mae, call that number back, we need to get an address and get an ambulance sent," he says. Mae's hand trembles as she dials Elliott's number. She shakes her head. "The line is busy, I will keep trying."

Steve decides to do something he has never done before in the twenty years he has worked in radio, he makes the decision to go 'off air' before the show is over. He fades up his mic and says "I truly hope everyone listening is Okay after what we all just heard. Please rest assured that one of our team is calling Elliott's number now, to check that an ambulance has been arranged. I hope Elliott's partner Michelle has managed to call for help and that she is alright. If you have been affected by what you have just heard please reach out to the following services." He presses a button and a list of phone numbers, text numbers, and websites are reeled off – The Samaritans, Mind, the radio station's online chat service, and email address, to name a few.

"I'm sorry to say, listeners, that I've had to make the difficult decision to end the show early, something I haven't ever had to do in all my years on radio. I think we all need to process what we have just heard. In twenty minutes Mike Mancini will be on air with his fabulous show 'Ten for Ten' – Ten songs at Ten PM. Please take care out there listeners. Good night." Steve takes his headphones off and places them on the desk. He looks up at Mae, who at the tender age of nineteen, has probably never experienced anything like this before. He can see that she is very stressed. "I will take over now love, you go and get yourself a glass of water. Has anyone answered the phone yet?" he asks.

Mae shakes her head solemnly, then stands and heads for the kitchen. "What the hell was that?" Dane says, finally finding his voice. "I don't know. The phone line is still engaged. All I can hope is that the wife is on the phone with the Ambulance service. Are you Okay Dane?"

"Just stunned mate. Thank you for handling that. I went to pieces."

"We all did our best given the circumstances," Steve says.

"Did she actually say he was bleeding from his eyes?" Dane asks. Steve nods. Mae walks back into the studio holding three glasses of water. She hands them out and the three of them sit in their seats silently. A few minutes later Mike Mancini walks in, to take over.

"Jesus Christ guys. I have no idea how to pick things up after all that," he says.

"Yeah, sorry it's going to be so difficult for you Mike!" Steve scoffs.

"The ratings are going to be screwed," Mike continues.

"Can you actually hear yourself, Mike? A bloke is out there dying and you're harping on about ratings?" Dane says. Mike stands by Dane, waiting for him to vacate his seat. "Unbelievable" Dane mutters. Mike doesn't even flinch. He begins setting up for his show, oblivious to the tension in the room.

"Steve, I will text you later. Mae, come on I will walk you to your car," Dane says.

"Thank you both, for tonight. I don't really know what else to say," Steve says quietly.

"See you tomorrow Steve," Mae says, then follows Dane out of the studio.

***

THREE DAYS LATER...

Dane lies in bed and begins his usual morning routine of checking his social media accounts and emails before making coffee. He checks the New Forest neighbourhood page on Facebook and the news he has been dreading is confirmed. **LOCAL MAN DIES AT HOME DURING RADIO INTERVIEW.** Dane clicks on the link for the local Newspaper's article. 'Thirty-eight-year-old Elliott Barnes is believed to have suffered a reaction to some new medication. The Father of two attacked his wife, before experiencing a fatal seizure. Sadly, his wife Michelle, died in hospital a few hours later. The NHS has urged anyone taking herbal medication from the company 'Happy You' to stop taking them right away and see a GP urgently. The medication, which has been advertised as being made from all-natural ingredients has taken America by storm and has garnered a following in the UK. The pills are said to be a natural alternative to antidepressants, however, over 300 similar cases of people dying from seizures have been reported in Texas, Los Angeles, New York, and Chicago. The World Health Organisation has launched an investigation and is recalling all 'Happy You' medication.'

"Shit!" Dane says out loud. He puts his phone on the bed, dresses, and then heads downstairs to make a cappuccino. While the machine hums away, and the silky brown liquid fills his mug, a siren noise blares from his phone. The screen flashes with a warning message **'NATIONAL EMERGENCY ALERT. DO NOT LEAVE YOUR HOMES. LOCK ALL DOORS AND WINDOWS. FIND A PLACE OF SAFETY IMMEDIATELY.'** The coffee machine is so loud, that he does not hear the siren.

He opens the bread bin and remembers that he forgot to pick up a loaf yesterday on his way home from the gym. He grabs his keys and his wallet from the centre island and heads out. During the short walk to the corner shop, he begins to feel uneasy. It is Friday and it is 8.30 a.m. The street should be full of cars with tired parents doing the school run and commuters who are late for work. There's no one standing at the bus stop, no postman delivering letters, and not a single dog walker in sight.

Dane opens the corner shop's door and steps inside. The shop is empty. There is no one standing behind the counter. He picks up a loaf of bread from the shelf and heads over to the till. He looks around impatiently. "Hello?" he calls out. Behind him, he can hear footsteps shuffling over. "At last" he mutters under his breath. The footsteps grow closer and his ears prick at the sound of groaning. He slowly turns to face the stranger behind him. The shop assistant walks forward, blood streaking down her cheeks like a crimson waterfall.

She holds her arms out towards Dane, gurgling as she tries to say something. "Jesus Christ!" Dane shrieks. He pushes his hand into the back pocket of his jeans, searching for his phone. "Shit!" he hisses, as he realises that he's left it at home. "Okay love, just relax, I am going to go and get some help," Dane says trembling. The woman lunges forward, grabbing at his jumper. Dane's back is pressed against the counter. He tries to bat her hands away, but she grabs his arm and sinks her teeth deep into his wrist. Dane pushes her with all the force he can muster, and she slumps onto the floor. "Fucking Hell!" he screams. The woman convulses on the floor. He watches in horror as her body stiffens, and her head twists to the side, her red eyes staring into his soul as she takes her last breath.

He feels nauseous as he tries to run home. He unlocks the front door, and staggers up the stairs, stopping halfway to clutch the banister. He sways on the step, feeling like he is about to faint. His breath is laboured as he finally reaches the bedroom. He grabs the phone from his bed. His eyes are blurry as he tries to focus on the screen. He presses 9 9 then freezes as he feels something wet running down his cheeks. He runs a hand across his face and looks down at his red palm, then staggers towards the ensuite. He slowly lifts his head to look into the mirror. He takes a deep breath as he braces himself for the convulsions. He watches for a few seconds as the foam builds at the corners of his open mouth, then falls to the floor.

July 20th 2007

Dear Tilly,

This letter is so difficult to write. I've drank some liquid courage and I've screwed up the previous four letters, but I need to get all of this off my chest, so here goes. If I don't say these things to you before tomorrow, I will spend the rest of my life wondering if things would ever have been different between us. Right now, you are probably hanging up your wedding dress, smoothing out the creases, and removing the shoes that we picked out together from the box.

Your stomach will be in knots right now, as you picture yourself exchanging vows with my brother Ben. I met you on Monday 23rd April 1995, my first day at Pine Hill Academy. It was love at first sight. You were the most popular girl in school. I envied your dark brown bob and chocolate button eyes. You were tall and slim, and the most confident fourteen-year-old I had ever met. I started at Pine Hill Academy halfway through Year nine. Mum and Dad had finally split up after years of arguments, and Mum decided that she needed a fresh start somewhere new. I didn't want to leave Birmingham and I had cried and cried when she said we were moving to

Monmouth. Didn't she understand that starting halfway through a school year was social suicide? I was leaving the very few friends I had, leaving a bustling city, to be a Billy no mates surrounded by fields and sheep.

No one wants to be the new kid. No one likes new kids. People think new kids are creepy and sad. And I was creepy and sad...Mrs Harrington had paired me with you that day so you could help me find my way around. Do you remember? You ran an inquisitive eye over me as I stood at the reception desk. My blazer was so new that it practically glowed, the badge was stiff and shiny, and there were still creases in the sleeves. I stood out like a sore thumb, there was an invisible sign around my neck saying 'NEW GIRL'.

My blonde hair was frizzy from the rain, I'd forgotten my umbrella, and as I looked at you, all happy and glamourous, I struggled to hold back tears. You were everything I wanted to be Til. I was chubby, spotty, shy, and awkward. Mrs Harrington told you my name was Zoe, and you said 'Don't worry Miss, me and Zoe are going to be best friends.' And we were. We *are*. I never told you this before, but on that day, when we first met, when you went to the toilet during lunch,

I picked your jumper up from your chair and sniffed it. I devoured your scent, Impulse body spray – Spirit was always your favourite, the one in the pink can.

I suppose that's when my obsession with you started. I went home that night and told Mum I wasn't hungry. I didn't want my tea, because I needed to lose weight, so I could look like you. I went to the local Asda and used my pocket money to buy some impulse, your scent, and sprayed it all around my bedroom. I couldn't wait to see you in school the next day, and I spent the evening listening to Sneaker Pimps and writing in my journal, gushing over my new best friend.

On June 1st I weighed myself and was pleased to see I had lost a stone. I still had a long way to go, before my body was anywhere near as perfect as yours. I'd been to Boots after school and bought a dark brown hair dye and some hair scissors. I cut my long hair, badly, I admit, and dyed it brown, just like yours. I couldn't change my blue eyes, but I was saving up my pocket money so I could buy some brown contact lenses. I spent ages in the bathroom, trying to copy the cat's eye flick you used to do with eyeliner. Mum caught me coming out of the bathroom and gasped. She said she was worried about how much weight I was losing and said she wanted to take me to see a Doctor. I told her to sod off. She asked me why I had changed my hair, and I told her I wanted to be someone else.

I knew you were shocked when you saw me at school the next day, but you were too polite to say anything. Kevin Reynolds pissed himself laughing when he walked into the form room for registration and saw my hair. He shouted 'Look at Tilly's creepy clone' and the whole class started laughing. You told him to sit down and be quiet, and at that moment, I wanted to throw my arms around you and kiss you in front of everyone.

All the boys at school fancied you Til, and you pretended to not notice. You've always been humble, and I love that about you. My world came crashing down that day I saw you kissing Ben. I couldn't breathe. I knew he had a crush on you, he was always asking me when you were next coming over for tea, and he could barely contain his excitement when Mum said you could come on holiday with us to Paris.

We went to Paris in August 1997, to celebrate our GCSE results. You passed everything, A's and B's across the board, I got three C's and failed everything else. You told me it didn't matter though, because we were always going to be best friends, and we were going to get part-time jobs at the same place and save our money to travel.

Ben had already done a year at college when we went to Paris. To me, he was my annoying older brother, but to you, he was an exciting art student, he was mature and cultured, and nothing like the boys our age, despite him only being eighteen months older. I would turn away when I saw you speaking to him so that you couldn't see the tears swell in my eyes. I used to want to hit him when he leaned in close to you and stared into your big brown eyes. And I hated seeing you twiddle your hair whenever he spoke to you.

I remember that afternoon in Paris like it was yesterday. We had lunch at a quaint little café, and sat outside on the terrace, drinking lemonade. Ben had a lager, Mum said he could have one because he wasn't that far off turning eighteen. Mum left us at the table to buy some earrings from a shop across the street. She'd had her eye on them for a couple of days, and protested that she couldn't afford them, but after a few glasses of wine she changed her tune, and said 'Sod it, you're a long time dead.'

I got up at the same time to go to the loo, and as I was weaving through the tables inside the restaurant, making my way back to our table I saw your heads locked together, and Ben's hands cupping your face. Was that your first kiss? Or had there been others? When I sat down, you both acted like nothing had happened. You asked me if I was okay, and said my face was really red. Ben laughed and said something about two minutes of sun is all it takes to turn me into a lobster. I wanted to pick my steak knife up and stab it into Ben's heart.

It wasn't long before you officially came out as a couple. I hated Ben so much, he had stolen my best friend. You spent all your time with him, and I only really saw you when you both had dinner at Mum's. You were both always out with other couples, and I was never invited. You went traveling together for six months in 1999, one of the things you said we would do together. Those six months were so lonely and painful. We spoke on the phone a handful of times, but our calls were very strained. The only thing we seemed to have in common back then was Ben.

You encouraged me to go on dates, and I did. I tried. I hated every single one. I've never thought of myself as gay. I am in love with a woman, yes, but I've never been attracted to other women, I've only ever been attracted to you. When you and Ben split up for a while in the summer of 2002, you came back to me for a few months. It was like old times, for a while. We were together every day. We went out dancing, watched films, and ate junk on the sofa, falling asleep together most nights. There was that one time when we both had too much to drink, and you told me you had always wondered what it would be like to kiss a woman. My heart raced, and I thought for a split second that you were going to kiss me, but you threw your head back and laughed. Minutes later you were sobbing about how much you missed Ben, and then seconds later you were sick everywhere. I cleaned you up, put you to bed, and lay next to you silently crying.

When you and Ben got back together and bought the house, I had to lose you all over again. I can count on my fingers the moments of real happiness in my life, and each one of them was spent with you. I went to shit when you and Ben moved in together. My eating disorder returned, I drank every night, and on my darkest days, I thought about ending it all. I should have told you years ago, how I felt. You are one of a kind Tilly. You are like sunshine. Your warmth and energy brighten up the darkest days. Your infectious laugh turns heads, and even though he's my brother, and I love him, Ben isn't good enough for you. When you called me excitedly, on March 18th, 2005, to tell me that Ben had proposed and you wanted me to be your Maid of Honor, I felt like I was going to die.

I started a relationship with Aaron, just to fill my time. You were so excited for me, and glad I had someone to bring to the wedding. You told me how happy you were that things were starting to fall into place. I don't love Aaron. I never have. I'm looking at my pale blue bridesmaid's dress right now. It is beautiful, you have always had good taste. I don't think I am going to be able to put it on. I don't think I am going to be able to follow you down that aisle in the morning.

I can't sit in the pews, and watch you get married. Til, I'm so sorry I feel this way. I'm sorry I'm like this. I am a freak. Giving you this letter will be the kiss of death. I know that. I know you'll never want to see me again. Ben will hate me too. All I've ever wanted is for you to just love me. Not in the way that you love a friend, but in the same way that I love you. I'm signing off now. I'm about to post this letter through your letterbox. I won't be there tomorrow. I'm sorry I have let you down. You are going to be the most beautiful bride, ever.

All my love, Zoe.

***

I wake up in agony. There's a pneumatic drill gnawing into my head. I turn my head to the side and see the two empty bottles of red wine on the bedside table. A wave of nausea washes over me. The letter. Oh Christ, the letter. I sit up far too quickly, clutching my head as I clamber out of bed. 'Please tell me you didn't post it, Zoe. Please!' I groan. I tip the bin upside down and unscrew the papers in there. There are four letters, but each of them only has a few lines, that have been scribbled out. The seven-page letter isn't in there. I start turning the room over, praying that I have just thrown it somewhere before I passed out cold.

I look at the alarm clock. It is 10.00 a.m. She will be up now, she will be getting ready. She will have read it by now. Hopefully, she will think it was just a wind-up. Who am I kidding? I grab my phone from the bedside table. No calls, no messages. I run to the toilet and throw up. Mid heave I hear a knock on the front door. *That will be Ben here to scream at me* I think to myself. I trudge down the stairs and lower my head as I open the door.

"I got your letter."

I lift my head and our eyes meet. I look away embarrassed and ashamed.

"Tilly. I…I don't know what to say."

"Is it true? Did you mean all that?" she asks.

"You need to go Tilly, you're getting married in three hours."

"Are you in love with me?" she asks. I nod.

"Why have you never told me this before? I mean how could you put all of that in a letter for me to read on the morning of my wedding?"

"I'm sorry," I whisper.

She takes both of my hands and squeezes them tightly. She stares into my eyes and smiles, then leans in and kisses me gently on the lips. I step back, confused and shocked.

"What are you doing?"

"Don't you get it Zo? I love you too. I always have."

"But what about Ben? And the wedding? Are you serious Tilly?"

"I love Ben too," she says.

"So what happens now? Are you going to go through with the wedding?" I ask.

"Yes Zoe, I am. I just came to tell you that I love you too, and to say goodbye."

"Goodbye?"

"I'm pregnant, I was going to tell you after the wedding. Me and you, these feelings we have for each other, they can't carry on. Especially now."

I blink through my tears. My world has shattered again. I watch her walk away. She stands at the bottom of the drive and turns to look at me one last time. She blows me a kiss, and then she is gone.

Printed in Great Britain
by Amazon